The Feather Merchants

Pinkhes the Peddler was a popular fellow in Chelm, not so much for the things he sold (just about all of it could be found in one shop or another), but because he brought back news of the outside world.

Returning from one of his trips, Pinkhes announced that a traveling circus was heading toward Chelm. The children had never been to a circus. Just the idea of seeing a real tiger or a camel was enough to set their heads spinning.

However, that dream was not to be, because Pinkhes also declared that under no circumstances should such a circus be allowed in Chelm.

When the children asked why, he said, "They were unkind, meanspirited, and anti-Semitic. Why, they called me all sorts of terrible names, names I wouldn't dare repeat lest my tongue turn to stone."

"Well, what did you do?" a little girl asked.

"I got my revenge," he said proudly. "I bought a ticket and I di

*For the gale children
in the Days of Foolishness*

THE
FEATHER
MERCHANTS

& Other Tales of the Fools of Chelm

✡

STEVE SANFIELD

Steve Sanfield

A Beech Tree Paperback Book
New York

10 9 8 7 6 5 4 3 2 1

Library of Congress Cataloging-in-Publication Data

Sanfield, Steve.
    The feather merchants & other tales of the fools of Chelm / by
Steve Sanfield
        p.   cm.
    Includes bibliographical references.
    Summary: Thirteen traditional European Jewish tales of the
town of Chelm and its silly citizens.
    ISBN 0-688-12568-9
    1. Legends, Jewish. [1. Folklore, Jewish. 2. Chelm, (Chelm,
Poland)—Folklore.] I. Title: Feather merchants and other tales
of the fools of Chelm. II. Title: Feather merchants.
[PZ8.1.S242Fe 1993]
398.2'089924—dc20
[E]   92-43767
                                                  CIP
                                                  AC

CONTENTS

אַ צעבראָכענער זייגער איז בעסער
ווי איינער וואָס גייט ניט ריכטיק:
אויף יעדן פֿאַל איז עס כאָטש ריכטיק צוויי מאָל אין טאָג.

A broken clock is still better
than one that goes wrong:
At least it's right twice a day.

The Feather Merchants

FOREWORD

ENJOY!
We'll talk later.

A Beginning

The Founding Fathers of Chelm looked out across the broad, flat valley below.

A wide river sparkled in the sunshine as it meandered slowly from east to west.

Like an immense pair of arms hugging a child in a snug embrace, soft, rolling hills encircled the valley on three sides.

Here and there chestnuts and maples mingled with birches and beeches, creating a dozen shades of dancing greenery.

And where the men stood, near the top of the mountain to the north, grew the towering pines and firs with which they planned to build their town.

After the proper prayers and ceremonies of dedication, they began their great work. They selected the largest and strongest trees. Nothing less would do. They carefully felled and limbed the sturdiest ones, but immediately a problem arose.

How were they to get these huge logs down to the valley?

The early Chelmites had no beasts of burden, no carts or wagons. All those would come later. But it is said, "When you must, you can," so the men simply lifted the logs onto their shoulders, a dozen to each, and, amid much huffing and puffing, they carried them down the mountain.

While all this activity was going on, a stranger happened to be passing through the valley. He watched in amazement as the men of Chelm struggled and wrestled with their heavy burdens.

"This is ridiculous," he said to himself. "These men are fools," which may have been the first time anyone ever applied that term to the good people of Chelm.

The stranger joined the workers up on the

mountain and suggested they try another way. He gave one of the logs a hearty kick, and it rolled down into the valley as if it knew exactly where it was going.

"Remarkable! A genius!" exclaimed the Chelmites. They immediately descended into the valley, hoisted the logs on their shoulders once more, and, with muscles straining and eyes popping, carried them back up the mountain. Then, one by one, they *rolled* their logs back down.

Chelm, as you probably already suspect, is a very special place, a place where remarkable things are always happening. It is a place where tears and laughter live close together, a place where kindness and sweetness and silliness fill the air.

Chelm is special because its people are special. They are like no others, for, you see, each and every Chelmite, regardless of position or vocation, is a Sage. They are all wise men and women. At least that's what they tell themselves.

That the rest of the world considers them

5

to be fools and simpletons does not bother them in the least. They know they are the wisest people on earth, and in the end, isn't that all that matters?

How, you may ask, did all these fools, or Sages, as the Chelmites prefer to call themselves, end up in one place?

A good question, but as is often the case when dealing with profound mysteries, there are many different explanations, none of which agree with one another. However, of the infinite number of possibilities, two stand out.

The first reminds us that the *Torah* says, "God watches over the simple." Now, in his boundless wisdom, knowing there is no way to predict what a simpleton may do, God gathered them all in one place so that it would be easier to keep an eye on them.

The second explanation, which is widely accepted by those who have given the matter serious consideration, is an old legend that tells us that, after God had created the world and everything upon it, there still remained two groups of souls to be distributed—those of the very, very wise and those of the very, very foolish.

It would be only fair to distribute such unique souls equally. Everywhere there were to be a few of the very wise and a few of the very foolish. This way every community would have those who might create problems and those who might solve them, even though one person's solution might well be another person's problem.

God prepared two separate sacks containing the souls of each. Then he instructed an angel to fly over the earth and leave a few from each sack here, a few from each sack there.

However, as the angel was flying over the high mountains just north of Chelm, he flew too close to the jagged peaks. The sack containing the foolish souls caught on a sharp outcrop and tore open. Down they poured into the valley below, where they have lived ever since.

The *Shul*

The most important single building in any Jewish town is the *shul*, or synagogue. It serves, not only as the House of Prayer and the House of Study, but also as a communal meeting place, so naturally it was the first structure to be built in Chelm.

The first men of Chelm started digging the *shul's* foundation, but a disturbing thought occurred to one of them.

"What," he asked, "are we going to do with all this dirt we're digging up? We can't just leave it here where we're going to have our *shul*."

"We never thought of that," declared the

others. "What, indeed, are we going to do with all this dirt?"

Many suggestions were made, but all were quickly rejected as unworkable.

"I have it!" shouted the same man who had posed the question in the first place. "All we have to do is dig a deep pit, and into it we'll shovel the dirt we're digging up for the foundation."

This suggestion was received with cheers, and the men began to dig another pit. They'd hardly broken the surface of the earth when someone else called out, "Wait a minute. This doesn't solve anything. What are we going to do with the dirt from this hole?"

The digging stopped as quickly as it had begun. Shovels hung in midair, for suddenly here was an entirely new problem: what to do with the dirt from the second hole?

It seemed like an impossible situation, but as would become the tradition in Chelm, an ordinary townsman saved the day. "It's really very simple," he said. "We'll just dig one more pit twice as large as this one, and into that we'll shovel all the dirt from this hole *and* all the dirt from the foundation."

There was no arguing with this early example of Chelmic logic, and the men returned to their work.

The building of the synagogue took the entire summer and a good part of the fall, but it was ready in time to celebrate *Rosh Hashanah*, the Jewish New Year. And what a grand celebration it was—a new synagogue, a new town, a new beginning.

As soon as the Days of Awe were over, everyone devoted all their energies to helping their neighbors finish their new homes. Doors were hung, roofs were covered, and by the time the first icy winds blew through the streets of Chelm, everyone was comfortably settled in their humble dwelling.

But that first winter was a difficult one, a very difficult one.

It arrived early and stayed late. Snow covered the ground for weeks at a time, often rising high enough to meet the icicles that hung down from the roofs. Cold chilled the bones until no one could even remember what it was like to be warm.

The little firewood that had been cut was soon gone. All that remained in the stoves and fireplaces were ashes, and ashes have never been known to keep anybody or anything warm. Shaking and shivering, people took to burning their own furniture, so that by the time the healing warmth of spring finally reached the valley, everyone was sitting on the floor.

It had been a terrible time. It was a miracle they all survived.

A town meeting was called. The prospect of another freezing winter was discussed, deliberated, and dissected. There was no dispute and no debate: everyone agreed that such discomfort should never be allowed to happen again. The solution? As simple as *aleph-beys*. The Chelmites built a high brick wall around the town to keep out the cold.

The Rabbi

Among the wisest of all Chelmites was the rabbi (would you expect anything less?), so wise, in fact, he often came up with answers to dilemmas that had nothing to do with the life of the spirit.

An example: a terrible occurrence. A thief had stolen the poor box from the synagogue. (Yes, Chelm had its thieves, just like every other town.) Who'd ever heard of such a thing—stealing money meant for the very poorest among the people?

What was to be done? Put up another poor box? The thief, if he'd been that desperate in the first place, would only steal it again. Not put one up? What kind of synagogue would it be without a poor box?

This was a serious problem indeed, but no problem was ever too difficult for the deep wisdom of the Chelmites, especially when many minds worked together. The directors of the synagogue held a meeting to examine the situation. They discussed, deliberated, and dissected, and it wasn't long before they arrived at a solution. A new poor box would be hung close to the ceiling, so high up that no thief, unless he could fly, would ever be able to reach it.

As the directors were congratulating themselves on their own sagaciousness, Berish the *Shammes*, who was responsible for the upkeep of the synagogue, pointed out that although no thief would be able to get at the poor box, neither would anyone else, thus making it impossible to leave a donation.

Here was an even more serious problem, since giving to charity was a joy and an honor as well as a duty.

Finally the rabbi stepped in and resolved

the quandary. A ladder would be built to allow the charitable to reach the poor box and leave their donations. And to prevent thieves from using it, a sign would be hung declaring,

> ONLY FOR THOSE WISHING
> TO MAKE DONATIONS
> NO THIEVES ALLOWED

Is it any wonder, then, that the people of Chelm put faith in their rabbi when it came to matters secular as well as spiritual? He was like the sages of old, always ready to help no matter how complicated the situation.

Baruch the Bookbinder once came to him and said, "Rabbi, my son, Yossel, is about to have his *Bar Mitzvah*. He has studied *Torah* and *Talmud*, the history of our people, the responsibilities that come with being thirteen. All this he knows well. He's about to reach his manhood, and I think I should tell him something about the birds and the bees, but I don't know what to say."

"First of all," the eminent rabbi replied, "forget about the birds and the bees."

"Forget about the birds and the bees? Why?"

"Because it's just not so."

"It's not so? But, Rabbi, how can you say that?"

"I can say it because it's true, and I know it's true because I proved it. You see, I too had always heard about the birds and the bees, but I wanted to see with my own eyes. I captured a bird and I captured a bee. Then I put them in a cage together for three days and three nights. I watched them constantly, and I tell you that nothing, absolutely nothing happened."

Yossel became *Bar Mitzvah*, and a few years later it was time for him to marry. In those days in Chelm, as elsewhere, it was still the custom to prearrange marriages. Parents would often make such decisions while their children were still very young, and sometimes the bride-and-groom-to-be did not actually meet until shortly before the wedding.

Such was the case here. Yossel was about to meet his future wife, Sossel, for the first time, and, being not particularly experienced in the ways of the world, he went to the rabbi to ask for some advice.

"Rabbi, I'm going to visit my Sossel tomorrow, but I have no idea of what to say to her. Can you help me?"

The rabbi smiled warmly and said, "It's simple, my boy. Men and women have been getting married since Adam and Eve, and very little has changed. When you see your fiancée, first talk to her about love. Then speak about family. And finally, finish up with a little philosophy. That should take care of everything."

Yossel thanked the rabbi and went on his way, all the time repeating the rabbi's advice, "Love, family, philosophy. Love, family, philosophy."

The next day, when he arrived at his intended's house, her parents were there to greet him. He couldn't very well speak of such intimate things in front of them, but as soon as the young couple was left alone, Yossel blurted out, "Tell me. Do you love noodles?"

"Yes, I love noodles," she answered, a little surprised. "Why shouldn't I love noodles?"

Yossel had no idea how to answer her question, so he said nothing. There was a long silence, and then he asked, "Tell me, do you have a brother?"

"No, I don't have a brother," she replied.

Ah, thought Yossel, *this is going to be easier than I thought. I've already taken care of love and family. Now, just as the rabbi told me, all I have to do is finish with a little philosophy.*

There was an even longer silence as Yossel strained for the right words. Finally he said, "Tell me, if you had a brother, would he love noodles?"

The rabbi's advice seemed to work, because Yossel did marry Sossel. But it wasn't long before he was back at the rabbi's, this time excited and clearly upset.

"Rabbi," he pleaded, close to tears, "you've got to help me. My wife just had a baby."

"Why, *mazel tov*," said the rabbi. "Congratulations. Children are the greatest joy of all. The pleasures they bring are more precious than gold. Besides, you're fulfilling the commandment: 'Be fruitful and multiply.' Why should you need my help?"

"You don't understand, Rabbi. We've been married only three months, and my mother told me herself that it takes a baby nine months to be born."

"My son," said the rabbi kindly, "your mother spoke the truth, but there is no problem that cannot be solved with the help of the proper logic properly applied. Now let me ask you a few questions. Have you lived with your wife for three months?"

"Yes, Rabbi."

"Has she lived with you for three months?"

"Yes, Rabbi."

"And you've lived together for three months?"

"Yes, Rabbi."

"Well, then. What's the total of three months plus three months plus three months?"

"Nine months, Rabbi."

"There!" the rabbi said. "Nine months, just as your mother told you. Now go home to your wife and child and rejoice."

Oyzar the Scholar

It is true that Chelm, from the first, was filled with Sages, and it's also true that remarkable things were always happening to them, but apart from that Chelm was not so different from any other town.

Chelmites were merchants and beggars, butchers and bakers, tailors and cobblers. They were drivers and drovers, woodcutters and water carriers, teachers and scholars.

Actually, because everyone was so wise to begin with, there were more scholars in Chelm than a pine tree has needles. However, among them was one who stood above the rest, one who was known to everyone as

The Scholar. His name was Oyzar—Oyzar the Scholar, to be precise.

Oyzar was well aware that in past generations the most respected members of the community, whether it be large or small, were the scholars. Who has not heard that "Learning is the best merchandise"? Yet it was neither riches nor respect that Oyzar desired. He simply loved analyzing and philosophizing—"dreaming," his wife called it. He spent his days and nights studying and thinking. He liked nothing better than to consider difficult and obscure problems that no one else had the time or inclination to approach.

For example, you already know that if you put sugar in a glass of tea (you probably use a cup, but in Chelm tea was always drunk from a glass) and then stir it until it dissolves, the tea, which is bitter to begin with, becomes sweet. This happens to be a fact of nature. It cannot be denied.

But have you ever asked yourself what is it that makes the tea sweet? Is it the sugar, or is it the stirring of the spoon? Before you answer too quickly and embarrass yourself, give some thought to the conclusion that Oyzar reached only after months of study and experimentation.

It is the stirring of the spoon.

Why add the sugar, then, you probably ask. A good question and one that many people have asked Oyzar. After all, if it's the spoon that's responsible for sweetening the tea, why waste the sugar by dissolving it? Well, according to Oyzar's calculations, you add the sugar so you'll know how long to stir the tea. Only when it's completely dissolved can you be sure the tea is sweet enough to drink.

Once, early in the springtime, just after the feast of *Purim*, Oyzar was busy trying to make sense of a curious question a young man named Shmuel had brought to him that very morning. Shmuel, although still a student (his secret ambition was to become a scholar and philosopher like Oyzar), was well past the age when he should have had a respectable beard, but no hairs grew on his chin, not a single one. He had a fine head of curly hair but no beard. His chin was as smooth as a newborn baby's.

"What could it be?" he asked Oyzar. "I'm strong and healthy. I eat well. I get plenty of rest, but no hair grows on my face like the other young men's. How can I become a true Sage like you if I don't have a beard like you?"

"True, all too true," said Oyzar, stroking his own bushy, gray beard. "Unless, of course, it's hereditary."

"No," said Shmuel, "that's impossible. My father and his father before him each had long, full beards that covered up half their bellies."

"Well, there must be a logical explanation," suggested Oyzar. "There always is. Why don't you let me think about it for a while? Come back this evening. Perhaps I'll have an answer for you."

Beardless Shmuel left Oyzar alone to ponder. The Scholar searched his books, but nowhere could he find a single clue to explain Shmuel's naked face.

Morning became afternoon, and as the day grew warmer Oyzar opened the window to cool his study and his mind. A soft breeze

23

entered. It carried with it the sweet scent of the first crocuses and the cleansing air of the season. It also carried the laughing voices of children playing under the window.

Oyzar was fond of children, and they of him. He spent much of his time with them, playing games and teasing them with riddles. On any other day he might well have joined them outside, but today their play was disturbing his concentration. He didn't want to hurt their feelings by telling them they weren't welcome around his house. Still, he had promised Shmuel an answer.

"Children," he called, leaning out the window. "Do you know what today is? Today is the day the great dragon of the sea is supposed to swim up our river."

The children stopped their romping. "Dragon? What dragon?" they asked, for as far as they knew no dragon had ever been seen in Chelm.

"The dragon of the sea," Oyzar explained. "He's twenty feet long, with the head of a lion and the body of a gigantic fish. He has the wings of an eagle and the horns of a bull.

He swims in the water and breathes fire and smoke. He travels all over the world, visiting every river once every hundred and twenty years, and today is the day he's supposed to come to ours. If you see him you will have good luck forever, but you'd better go quickly or the dragon will have already swum past Chelm."

The children needed no further encouragement. Off they ran to the river, laughing all the way, and Oyzar settled down determined to find an answer to Shmuel's dilemma.

He had barely begun when he was disturbed by the shouting of a crowd of people rushing after the children. "Where are you all going in such a hurry?" he asked from his window.

"To the river, to the river," someone yelled. "Haven't you heard? There's a fire-breathing dragon there that comes only once in a man's lifetime."

For a moment Oyzar the Scholar was tempted the join the crowd. When else might he have a chance to see such a creature? But then he remembered that he himself had made up the story to get the children to leave him in peace and quiet. He shook his head in wonder over the power of a simple rumor.

He'd barely sat down at his desk again when he heard another commotion in the street below his window. It was the entire Council of Seven Sages and their families hurrying toward the river.

"Where are you all off to?" Oyzar called.

"To the river to see the dragon," replied one of the Sages. "Come quickly. There's a huge dragon who devours lions and eagles but gives his blessing to people."

Oyzar grabbed his coat and ran into the street. *Who knows?* he thought to himself. *If even the Council of Seven Sages, the wisest of the wise, believes there's a dragon in the river, it's probably so, and I wouldn't want to be the only one to miss it.*

By the time he reached the river, everybody else was on their way back to town. Most were grumbling and shaking their heads because there was no dragon to be seen anywhere. This didn't discourage Oyzar, however. He wasn't called The Scholar for nothing. A true scholar must prove everything for himself. Otherwise there is no way to know for certain whether something is true or not.

But, alas, even for Oyzar there was no dragon.

As he walked slowly home, he speculated about how such a wild rumor could have got started, but since there was no simple explanation forthcoming, Oyzar moved his mind to the pressing matter of Shmuel's beard, or rather the lack of it.

By the time he arrived back in his study, Oyzar had penetrated the mystery. When Shmuel returned later that evening, Oyzar was ready for him.

"It's clear," Oyzar began, "that your lack of a beard is hereditary."

"Hereditary? How could that be?" Shmuel asked, bewildered. "We both know that my father and my grandfathers all had healthy beards just like everybody else."

"That is true," Oyzar said gently, "and most boys take after their fathers, but you, you must take after your mother."

"That's it!" exclaimed Shmuel, delighted

with the news. "I must take after my mother, since she has no beard."

And Shmuel went on his way grateful for the explanation and surer than ever that when he grew up he wanted to be just like The Scholar.

Later that year, near the end of summer when the days are long and the dust sits heavily upon the roads, Oyzar's wife, Perl, went to visit her sister on the far side of Chelm. Knowing her husband to be the dreamer he was, Perl gave him very specific and, she thought, very clear instructions.

"If the baby begins to wake up, rock the cradle slowly and she'll go right back to sleep. If the *tsimmes* starts to boil over, move it to the back of the stove until it cools down a bit."

"No need to worry," said Oyzar. "If the baby wakes, rock her. If the *tsimmes* boils, move it."

Confident that her husband understood, Perl went out the door, but not a minute had passed and she was back. She'd remembered the jar of black currant preserves she had made only a few days before. She'd also remembered Oyzar's sweet tooth, almost as famous in Chelm as his penetrating wisdom. She wanted to serve the preserves on *Rosh Hashanah* when they wished each other a sweet year. What she didn't want was Oyzar devouring them all.

"Oyzar, my love," she said gently. "I forgot to tell you. Be sure not to touch the fruit jar there on the shelf. It's filled with rat poison."

"If the baby wakes, rock her. If the *tsimmes* boils, move it. Don't touch the jar—it's poison. It's all simple enough," Oyzar reassured her. "Give my best to your sister, and don't worry about a thing."

Perl left and Oyzar went to his study, planning to think his way through a situation that had presented itself the night before in a dream. "Suppose," he began, talking to himself, "all the men in Chelm became one gigantic man, bigger even than Goliath, and then suppose . . ." But he couldn't complete his speculation, because what began to run through his mind were Perl's instructions: "If the baby wakes, rock her. If the *tsimmes* boils, move it. Don't touch the jar—it's poison."

This was an impossible situation. The baby was in the bedroom, the *tsimmes* was in the kitchen, and the jar was in the pantry. How could he possibly keep an eye on everything when everything wasn't in the same place? If he were to spend the morning worrying about such things, he'd never be able to do his own work.

A scrunching of the brow and a squinting of the eyes gave Oyzar his resolution. First, he dragged his own rocking chair from his study to the kitchen. Then he moved the cradle in front of the stove and set the fruit jar on the table next to it. Finally—and this is where he revealed his true genius—he tied one end of a rope to the cradle and the other end to his ankle. From his chair he could now watch the *tsimmes*, rock the cradle, and meditate on his original problem all at once, which is exactly what he did.

Suppose all the men in Chelm became one gigantic man and all the trees on the mountain joined together to become one stupendous tree and all the rivers and lakes and streams somehow flowed together to become one limitless lake. . . .

The sweet *tsimmes* simmered slowly on the stove. The baby slept the sleep only the innocent know. And Oyzar slipped deeper and deeper into his own reverie.

Then suppose this gigantic man picked up a massive ax that had been made from all the axes in the world and proceeded to chop down that stupendous tree, which would then fall into that limitless lake—is there anyone who would be able to imagine the size of the splash it would make?

Such was Oyzar's fantasy . . . and when, after an hour or more, that man finished chopping that tree, which fell into the middle of that lake, the resulting splash in Oyzar's mind was as real as the tongue in his mouth.

With a shout he leaped out of his chair. It turned over. The rope attached to his ankle pulled the cradle, knocked it on its side, and dumped the baby onto the floor.

Oyzar rushed to pick up the baby, who was

now shrieking and screaming, but he smashed into the cradle, crashed into the stove, and upended the pot of *tsimmes*, which spilled across the top of the stove and immediately commenced to burn.

This was a disaster, a catastrophe greater than the fall of that gigantic tree.

"Oy, oy, oy, oy," Oyzar moaned. "My wife will never forgive me. Who knows what she'll do?"

There was only one thing for Oyzar to do, and he did it.

When Perl returned, she could scarcely believe the scene that awaited her. The baby lay on her stomach on the floor, bawling and blubbering, her eyes red from tears. The cradle was splintered, its pieces scattered about. The rocking chair, which didn't even belong in the kitchen, lay askew on its side. The fruit jar, which also didn't belong there, was tipped on the table without its cap. The entire house was filled with the nose-wrinkling odor of burned carrots and prunes from the spilled *tsimmes*, which had bubbled and hardened on the stove.

And where was her husband, the esteemed scholar?

He was nowhere to be seen amid this chaos.

Perl heard a low moan from the bedroom, and when she looked, there he was lying in bed with the covers pulled up to his chin. His skin was pale, almost gray, and he had a sad, faraway look in his eyes.

"You *schlemiel*! You fool!" Perl screamed. "I leave you alone for a few hours and you destroy everything. You're worthless. You're worse than good-for-nothing. Look at you lying there in bed as if everything were fine. I should strangle you."

"Shh, please," begged Oyzar. "Speak softly. You won't have to strangle me, although God knows I deserve it. I'll be dead soon anyway."

"Dead? What are you babbling about now?"

"Well," Oyzar continued, "when I saw what I had done, although I'm not exactly sure how it happened . . . You see, there was this enormous splash. . . ."

"Splash? What splash, you idiot!"

"It doesn't matter. It's too late now. When

I saw what had happened, I knew you'd never forgive me. I couldn't live with that, so I ate all the poison in the fruit jar, and now I'm dying."

There was nothing Perl could say, at least nothing that would do any good—not that day nor for many days after.

Of course, Oyzar didn't die. Eventually Perl forgave him. He was her husband, and she did love him. He was, after all, The Scholar.

The *Mikva*

The Founding Fathers of Chelm concluded that if their town was going to take its proper place among others of the world, more public buildings were needed. The Chelmites were justifiably proud of their synagogue, but it wasn't quite enough.

After serious consideration, it was decided that a *mikva*, a ritual bathhouse, should come next, so that prior to each Sabbath, holiday, or special occasion, everyone would be able to bathe correctly.

Once again the men climbed the mountains and felled some of the larger trees. This time, however, they needed no one to show them the best way to get the logs down the slope. They simply gave each one a healthy kick, and just as the trees had done years before, these too rolled to the bottom without having to be told where to go.

But once at the bottom, it was not to be so simple, because Dovid the Barrelmaker asked which end should be carried into town first.

"What do you mean, which end? What difference does it make?" one of the men asked.

"What difference does it make?" Dovid responded. "It makes all the difference in the world. Correct me if I am mistaken, but I believe each of these logs has two ends."

Who could argue? Everyone could see with his own eyes that each log did indeed have two ends.

Dovid continued, "It is well known that the one who goes first is the one most honored, and since we have already honored these logs by choosing them above all others to use in our *mikva*, we must now decide which end should be further honored by being carried into town first."

Of course, this observation made perfect

sense to everyone, and a discussion began about which end should be so honored. Those who were right-handed naturally thought it should be the right end, and, just as naturally, those who were left-handed thought it should be the left end.

"Right." "Left." "Right." "Left." "Right." "Left."

Because there were just as many left-handed folk in Chelm as right-handed folk, the debate continued through the afternoon. With darkness gathering, they could see that soon they would be unable to see. They could also see that they were no closer to an agreement than when they started.

Hoping a wisdom more penetrating than their own might settle the matter, they took their problem to Oyzar the Scholar.

"If only all problems were as simple as this one"—Oyzar sighed—"how pleasant life would be. All you need to do is cut off the left end of the log. Then you will have only one end, the right end, and that being the only end left, it will be the right end to carry into town first."

"Another brilliant solution by our distinguished scholar," Dovid declared, and the men returned to their homes that night with easy minds. They met early the next day ready to follow Oyzar's advice and continue with the work of building the bathhouse.

Because it had been Dovid who was the first to realize that honor was not for human beings alone, and because as a barrelmaker he had a lifetime of experience with wood, he was given the honor and responsibility of cutting off the left end of the first log.

He took up his saw and began while his comrades watched. Forward and back and forward again the saw flashed in the morning sun. Sawdust flew, and the tangy scent of pine sap filled the air. The saw cut through the wood, and a thin round fell to the ground. The men cheered, but when they looked closely they saw the log still had two ends. Once again they could not deny what their eyes told them.

"Perhaps you haven't cut off enough," suggested one, and Dovid began again. His saw slid back and forth until another round fell from the log.

Another cheer, but still the log had two ends.

It is written that "where men truly wish to go, there their feet will carry them," and Dovid was not to be put off so easily. With fierce determination, he cut round after round until he was too weary even to lift his saw. Another man took over, and he too cut round after round, but no matter how many ends were cut off, two ends still remained—even though they were now separated by less than a foot of wood.

This would never do. Foot-long logs might be well and good to build a dollhouse, but a bathhouse—never. So back they went to Oyzar the Scholar with their new dilemma.

Oyzar, ever ready to help his fellow man, came to look at the logs. When he saw the tiny stub of a log, he realized they could cut end after end forever, but there would still be no end to two ends.

"There is no need to cut further," he announced. "All you have to do is carry these logs breadthwise into town. That way both ends will be first, and both will be honored equally."

Oyzar's solution had overcome their difficulty, but as soon as the men began to carry the logs, they saw they were faced with still another predicament. The road into town, lined with houses, was far too narrow for the length of the logs.

This time the men took it upon themselves to find a solution. They didn't want Oyzar or anyone else, God forbid, to think of them as fools. They simply tore down the buildings on both sides of the road, then proceeded to carry the logs to the bathhouse site. The houses would have to be rebuilt, of course, but that would have to come later. After all, even angels can't sing two songs at once.

For now, the quandary of which end of the logs to honor had been resolved.

Eventually the *mikva* was completed, and a lovely bathhouse it was. Only the most polished stones from the river were used to line the sides of the men's and women's tubs. Rich red tiles from Kuzmer covered the roof, and set high in the walls were thick beveled windows from Bialystok through which the rays of the afternoon sun became a thousand rainbows that danced on the pools below.

Everything was in place except the benches. They still had to be built, and it was about these unbuilt benches that a discussion began. The discussion became a debate and the debate became a dispute, because there were some who thought the benches should be smooth while others thought they should be rough.

The smoothniks, as they were called, claimed that if the benches weren't sanded smooth, everyone would leave the bathhouse with tiny splinters in their you-know-whats, and that would never do.

That might be true, agreed the roughniks, as the opposition was called, but a few splinters would be much less harmful than the slipping and sliding that was sure to occur if the benches were sanded smooth. Once the wood got wet, and there was no question that it would get wet in a bathhouse, the benches would become as slick as fresh ice, and the slipping and sliding would begin.

When people slip and slide, someone's sure to fall, and when someone falls, someone's bound to bump his head, and when someone bumps his head, someone's likely to get knocked out, and if someone is knocked out, someone's probably not going to wake up, and if someone doesn't wake up, it'll mean that someone has died, and if someone dies, it'd be a far greater tragedy than having a few people walk around with splinters in their you-know-whats.

"Ridiculous," countered the smoothniks. "The benches in every bathhouse in the world are smooth."

"This bathhouse is not every bathhouse," countered the roughniks. "This is Chelm's bathhouse."

And so the dispute went, back and forth, back and forth, until a compromise was reached: the benches were properly sanded, but to keep people from slipping and sliding they were set with the smooth side down.

Pinkhes the Peddler

There lived in Chelm a man who spent as much time away from his home as he did at it. His name was Pinkhes, and he was a peddler by trade. He would travel to all the surrounding towns and villages, offering his wares for sale.

"Pots and pans," he would call out. "Pots and pans for sale," and everyone would know the peddler had arrived. His sack was always filled to overflowing, and not just with pots and pans. There would be cups and dishes, spools of thread, bolts of cloth, even a piece of used clothing now and then. For the young girls there were bits of brightly colored ribbon and amber beads from the Baltic Sea. For the boys there were spinning tops or maybe a tiny carved wooden bear Pinkhes had picked up somewhere in the dark forests of the Ukraine.

Sometimes Pinkhes traveled in a rickety wagon that squeaked and creaked. It was pulled by a broken-down horse who also squeaked and creaked, but sometimes the horse was too weak or too hungry or too dead to go anywhere. On those days Pinkhes would fill his sack with as much as he could carry and set off on foot.

Once he was trudging home after selling hardly anything when a kindhearted farmer stopped and offered him a ride in his hay-filled wagon.

Pinkhes politely accepted the offer, climbed up on the wagon, and sat down beside the farmer, all the time keeping his sack slung over his shoulder. The farmer giddyapped his horse, and off they went.

A mile down the road, Pinkhes still had not put down his sack. The farmer thought it odd but said nothing. He figured his passenger would do so once he felt at ease, but after a few more miles Pinkhes still had his heavy sack hanging over his back.

Unable to contain himself any longer, the farmer asked, "Why don't you put your sack down in the wagon? Surely you'd be more comfortable that way."

"You're probably right," answered Pinkhes, "but I also have a horse and know how hard they must work, poor creatures. Your horse is kind enough to carry me, and I'm grateful. I wouldn't want to add my load to his burden."

Pinkhes the Peddler was a popular fellow in Chelm, not so much for the things he sold (just about all of it could be found in one shop or another), but because he brought back news of the outside world. With few exceptions, most Chelmites spent their lives close to Chelm, but Pinkhes was always crossing rivers and mountains that most townsfolk had never heard of, never mind seen.

Returning from one of his trips, Pinkhes announced that a traveling circus was heading toward Chelm. The children had never been to a circus. Just the idea of seeing a real tiger or a camel was enough to set their heads spinning.

However, that dream was not to be, because Pinkhes also declared that under no circumstances should such a circus be allowed in Chelm.

When the children asked why, he said, "They were unkind, meanspirited, and anti-Semitic. Why, they called me all sorts of terrible names, names I wouldn't dare repeat lest my tongue turn to stone."

"Well, what did you do?" a little girl asked.

"I got my revenge," he said proudly. "I bought a ticket and I didn't go in."

Once, at the approach of the Sabbath, Pinkhes found himself in Berdichev. He was a long way from home, and even if he'd had two fleet-footed stallions harnessed to his wagon instead of his old nag, he never would have reached Chelm in time to welcome the Sabbath angels with his family. He decided to spend the night where he was.

He arrived at the Berdichev synagogue a

little early and stood by the stove, warming himself while he waited for the evening prayers to begin. The *shammes* noticed him and, wanting to make this stranger feel comfortable, engaged him in conversation.

"Do you like riddles?" he asked.

"Oh, I love riddles," answered Pinkhes.

"Well, here's one for you," said the *shammes*. "Who am I? I am my father's son, but I am not my brother."

"That's it?" Pinkhes asked.

"That's it."

"I am my father's son, but I am not my brother. I am my father's son, but I am not my brother. I am my father's son, but I am not my brother," Pinkhes repeated again and again.

He stretched his mind as far as it would go, but no solution presented itself. "All right," he said, "I give up. Who is it?"

"Why, it's me!" announced the *shammes*.

Ah, what a wonderful riddle, thought the peddler. He was delighted with its cleverness and could scarcely wait to share it with his friends back in Chelm.

When he returned home a few days later, he wasted no time. He assembled his fellow Sages and told them, "I have a wonderful riddle for you, but it is very difficult, so difficult, in fact, I doubt whether even your combined wisdom can answer it. Are you ready?"

"We're ready. We're ready."

"Here it is. I am my father's son, but I am not my brother. Who am I?"

First there was a silence, then a murmur, finally a steady drone as if a hive of bees had just entered the room. "I am my father's son, but I am not my brother. I am my father's son, but I am not my brother," the Sages repeated. Brows were scrunched, eyes were squinted, fingers were pointed at temples as they went on reciting the riddle. "I am my father's son, but I am not my brother. I am my father's son, but I am not my brother."

Again and again and again the riddle was intoned until finally, in unison, they said, "We give up. Tell us. Who is it?"

"Why, it's the *shammes* at the Berdichev synagogue," Pinkhes said triumphantly.

"And," he added, "if you don't believe me, I can have him come here and tell you himself."

Pinkhes once traded a batch of his own goods for a load of oats, which he drove to the marketplace in his wagon.

A merchant approached and asked, "What are you selling today?"

Pinkhes looked behind him at his horse and wagon, covered his mouth with his hand, and whispered softly into the merchant's ear, "Oats."

"Oats?" asked the man, surprised. "If you're selling oats, why does it have to be a secret?"

"Shh, shh," whispered Pinkhes. "Not so loud, please. I don't want my horse to know."

Yossel and Sossel

Chelm was not the wealthiest town in the world. Oh, there were rich men, but none to brag about as you might about a Rothschild or a Rockefeller, and because even a peeled grape does not fall into your mouth without help, everyone had to work—whether they wanted to or not.

Some men were forced to seek employment in the neighboring towns and cities beyond the valley. Most found work close enough so they could return to their homes and families each week to observe the Sabbath. Most, that is, but not Yossel.

Yossel, whose family had grown to five children, took a position teaching others' children in Kotsk. Kotsk was less than half a day's journey from Chelm; yet Yossel returned home only once a year. That was each spring, when he came back to Chelm to celebrate the eight days of Passover.

Because family life is such a treasure, the teacher's continual absence troubled the rabbi. It didn't seem right that a man should be separated from his wife and children for most of the year. He called Yossel to him and asked him about the situation.

"Yossel, dear Yossel, there is something about your life that disturbs me deeply."

"But, Rabbi, what could disturb you? It was you who told me that teaching is an honorable profession."

"True, Yossel, true. The teaching of children is as important as any prayer. That is not what bothers me. It is the fact that you come home to your own children and your wife only once a year. It's not as if you were working in another country. You're close enough to join your family every *Shabbes*."

"Every *Shabbes*?" Yossel protested. "Rabbi, you don't realize what it is you're asking me to do. Every *Pesach* I come home, and every *Chanukah*, nine months later, my wife has another baby. Do you know what would happen if I came home every week?"

After the rabbi's elucidation, and his own consideration, Yossel saw the truth of his situation. He followed the rabbi's counsel and acquired a teaching position in Chelm.

One autumn, shortly after *Yom Kippur*, he went to visit some of his relatives in Dubno, across the Bug River. He hadn't been gone a week when a messenger brought Sossel this letter:

> *Greetings to my wonderful wife.*
> *All is well so far, and I pray the same is true for you. The cold autumn winds are beginning to blow here. I send this letter because I want you to send me your slippers. I say your slippers instead of my slippers, because if I said my slippers, you would read my slippers and send me your slippers, and that would never*

*do because I would end up with your
slippers and you would end up with
my slippers, and one pair would be
too big and one pair would be too
small. Therefore, I say your slippers
so that you'll read your slippers and
send me my slippers. I greet the children and send my blessings.*

Your faithful husband,

Yossel

Sossel read the letter only once and immediately sent Yossel his slippers, proving, not
that anyone ever doubted it, that the women
of Chelm were equal in their wisdom to their
men.

Shortly after his return from Dubno, Yossel
was sitting at the kitchen table writing a letter
by the light of a single kerosene lamp. Sossel
joined him and noticed that he was making

unusually large letters, so large, in fact, that he could fit no more than a few words on each sheet of paper.

"Who are you writing to?" she asked.

"My uncle in Dubno."

"But why are you making such large letters?"

"Because," answered Yossel, "may it never happen to you or me, he's deaf."

"I'm sorry he's deaf, but what does that have to do with the size of the letters?"

"Oh, he can't read," Yossel explained, "so whoever reads this to him will know to read it loud enough so he'll be able to hear."

Berish the *Shammes*

As the caretaker of the synagogue, Berish the *Shammes* stood at the center of communal life. He was not only expected to keep the synagogue clean and the prayer books and ceremonial objects in good repair, he was also responsible for keeping the heat in and the rain out.

When a sundial was donated and a rainstorm drenched it, it was Berish who built a roof to cover it so the dial wouldn't be ruined by getting wet.

But his responsibilities went far beyond maintenance and cleaning. It was Berish who announced the time for prayer each day and the time of the Sabbath bath each week. He collected synagogue dues, carried messages for the rabbi, and, in the end, made everyone's funeral arrangements.

Once there was a dreadful accident in the marketplace. Meyer the Driver had gotten his wagon stuck deeply in the mud. Just as his horse was pulling it free, Meyer slipped under the wheels and was killed instantly.

His wife, Rifke, had to be told, so the rabbi turned to his trusted aide for this delicate task.

"Berish," he instructed him, "I want you to go to Rifke and tell her that her husband has been killed, but I want you to break the news to her as gently as possible. Do you understand?"

"Don't worry, Rabbi," Berish assured him. "I'll be as gentle as a mother with a newborn baby."

The *shammes* set off immediately for Meyer's house. He knocked, and a woman came to the door.

"Good afternoon. Could you tell me if the Widow Rifke lives here?" he asked.

"I'm Rifke and I live here," she replied, "but I'm not a widow."

"Ho, ho, ho," chuckled Berish. "How much do you want to bet?"

One of Berish's weekly tasks was to walk through Chelm each Friday afternoon, just before the sun began to set, alerting all the merchants that it would soon be time for them to close their shops and prepare for the Sabbath.

It happened that one Friday, early in the winter, the first snow fell. It began late in the morning and continued well into the afternoon. By the time it stopped, it seemed as if the entire town had been wrapped in a white prayer shawl. The snow covered the muddy, rutted streets and the smoke-stained roofs of the houses. Everything looked so fresh and new it dazzled the eye.

The rabbi, taking a rest from his studies, was gazing out the window at the sparkling landscape when a disturbing thought jolted him from his reverie. It would soon be time for Berish to make his rounds. To do so, he would have to tread upon the pure snow, leaving dirty tracks behind him wherever he went.

The rabbi's love and appreciation of natural beauty ran so deep that he wanted everyone else in Chelm to enjoy it also. What to do? What to do?

Another problem—but to the rabbi such matters were like a loaf of freshly baked pumpernickel to a starving man. He simply rested his elbows on his desk, scrunched up his brow, squinted his eyes, pointed his index finger at his temple, and thought.

Even before a hungry man could devour that loaf, the rabbi knew what must be done to keep the *shammes* from marring the beauty of the newly fallen snow. Berish should stand on a table so his feet would not disturb so much as a flake. Then four strong men would each grab a leg and carry the table with Berish on it throughout the town.

So well did this plan work that, to the delight of all true lovers of beauty, it became one of Chelm's most enduring traditions.

Old age comes to us all and so it did to Berish. As he began to lose his hair, he also began to lose some of his strength. He was no longer robust as he had once been, and it became more and more difficult for him to trudge through the streets of town each day, banging on the shutters to call the people to morning prayers.

As soon as the situation came to the rabbi's attention, he knew that something had to be done. To ask Berish to continue with this task would be most unkind, but to replace him with someone else would be more than unkind. It would be an insult, since no one likes to be told they're too old to do what they did only yesterday.

In the end it was the rabbi's infinite wisdom, kindness, and loyalty to his *shammes* that led to the solution: henceforth, all the shutters from all the houses would be stored in the synagogue courtyard, where Berish could bang them without straining himself by having to walk around the town.

A Celebration

When little Esther was born, her father, Reb Gershon, one of Chelm's most prosperous merchants, was filled with joy and swelled with pride. To celebrate the birth of his first daughter, he invited, not only his immediate family and closest friends, but also the most eminent citizens of Chelm. "Please come and eat and be merry in honor of my daughter, Esther," said the invitation.

His house was crowded with guests. The tables were covered with snow-white linen cloths, and on the tables were dozens of jugs of water, a dozen dozen at least, surrounded by hundreds of crystal glasses.

Reb Gershon greeted everyone. Everyone congratulated him. Some brought gifts for Esther. People talked politely with one another while they waited for the feast to begin. They talked and waited and talked some more, until it became clear that nothing but water would be served.

One of the elders finally took it upon himself to ask, "Reb Gershon, what's going on here? You invite us to a feast to celebrate your daughter's birth, and all you're serving is water? What kind of a feast is that?"

"But water's the very best thing I could possibly serve," Reb Gershon replied proudly.

When he saw the blank stares on everyone's face, he continued, "You see, I had decided that nothing would be too good for this feast, so yesterday I went to the fish market and asked for the finest fish available. The fishmonger said, 'I have some fish here that are as sweet as sugar,' so I thought to myself that sugar must be better than fish.

"I went to the grocer and asked for sugar, and he boasted that his sugar was as sweet as honey, so naturally I assumed that honey would be better than sugar. I asked for honey, and he told me that his was as pure as olive oil.

"Well, I figured that oil must be better than honey, so I asked if he had any. Just as he started to fill a bottle, he assured me, 'This oil pours like water.' I didn't need anyone to convince me that water must certainly be better than oil.

"I mean, since sugar is better than fish, and honey is better than sugar, and oil is better than honey, and water is better than oil, then water must be the very best of all. And since all of you have honored me by coming here to celebrate the birth of my daughter, should I insult you by serving anything less than the best?"

No one could dispute such remarkable reasoning, and everyone raised their water-filled crystal glasses in a joyous toast, "*L'chayim!* To life! To Esther!"

The Inn of the
Stolen Moon

On the eastern edge of
Chelm, just inside the gate, beside the road
that leads out into the world and back again,
stands a large, rambling, two-story wooden
building. Behind it is a group of sheds and
stables, each one of which leans crazily in its
own direction, and in front, hanging from a
pine post, is a sign so faded that it can be read
only if the person reading it already knows
what it says.

THE INN OF THE TWO BROTHERS, pro-
claims the sign, and although it's true that the
brothers Avrom and Reuven are its owners,
everyone in Chelm calls the place THE INN
OF THE STOLEN MOON. Let me explain.

Avrom and Reuven wanted to be rich. Actually it was more that they were tired of being poor. As is the case with many poor dreamers, not only in Chelm but throughout the world, the brothers spent more time thinking about work than doing it, the result of which was, they remained poor.

For example, they once considered selling bagels, but that would mean baking them, and baking them, as any baker can testify, means work. Baking bagels was out of the question. They thought they'd found an easy way to riches when Avrom suggested that, instead of selling the bagels themselves, they sell the holes that go in the middle of the bagels.

"Every bagel baker needs holes. A bagel without a hole is no bagel at all," he proclaimed.

Reuven agreed wholeheartedly. "Without a hole, a bagel is just a roll."

Try as they might, however, they could not discover a source for the holes, and that proposal, like so many others, had to be abandoned.

* * *

It was an earlier and far more ambitious scheme, however, that had changed the name of the inn in everyone's mind from The Inn of the Two Brothers to The Inn of the Stolen Moon.

Avrom and Reuven knew that, during *Rosh Chadosh* at the beginning of every month, in villages and towns like their own, Jews observed a special ceremony to welcome the new moon. When the first slim silver crescent reappeared after nights lit only by stars, the people would leave the synagogue, go into the fields, and say the Blessing of the New Moon.

It was a practice that had been followed for as long as anyone could remember, and was as important a part of everyone's life as the lighting of the candles each week to welcome the Sabbath.

Without the moon, reasoned the brothers (and who could argue?), the blessing would be impossible. If someone could capture the moon and keep it in Chelm, then Jews from all over the world would have to travel to

Chelm in order to perform the ceremony. If that someone who now owned the moon were to charge a small fee to use the moon, a fee that even a beggar could afford, say a *zloty* or two, then each month those *zlotys* would be sure to add up to a substantial sum.

And further, if that someone also happened to own the only inn in Chelm (as did the brothers—"Aha!"), the only place visitors could stay and take their meals, then that someone would soon be wealthy beyond measure.

After such a brilliant analysis of the situation, all that remained was for Avrom and Reuven to make this dream a reality. Although they preferred idleness and leisure to actual labor, the promise of such great wealth was so alluring, the brothers wasted no time in putting their plan into action.

Now, the moon, especially when it's full, loves water. Whenever the full moon is out and about on its journey across the heavens, it always stops to refresh itself in bodies of water: ponds, lakes, streams, quiet eddies in a river, even the countless mud puddles that mark the roads in spring and fall. The moon never fails to visit them all—if only for a moment. As they say in Chelm, "Even a blind man can see that."

All the brothers had to do was create their own body of water, one that could be sealed tight, so when the moon came to visit, it couldn't escape.

Dovid the Barrelmaker supplied the barrel, complete with a lid, and Simon the Water Carrier filled it with water from his buckets. Avrom and Reuven had what they needed. It seemed that capturing the moon was going to be as simple as eating honey with a spoon on a hot summer day.

The brothers said nothing to anyone, not wanting to share their perfect plan, or their perfect profits. They hid the barrel in one of the old, unused sheds behind the inn and waited patiently for the full moon to return to Chelm.

It wasn't long before the moon appeared in all its glory. The brothers were ready. They dragged the barrel outside and removed its lid. They themselves hid quietly in the shadows, holding their breath, not daring to speak, lest the moon become suspicious and run away before it could be captured.

Slowly the moon glided through the night sky, bathing the world below in its cool, soft glow. When it was directly above the barrel, it dropped into the water to take a sip. Avrom and Reuven rushed forward, covered the barrel with the lid, and nailed it shut so the moon had no way out.

All had gone according to their plan. The moon was theirs. Soon they would be rich men.

A few days before the beginning of the month of *Tammuz*, the brothers started spreading word that they now owned the moon, but being of generous natures, they'd be willing to make it available to anyone—for a small rental fee, of course. When the other Chelmites heard about this, they thought it must be some kind of joke they couldn't understand, a riddle perhaps. Who ever heard of anyone owning the moon? But all Avrom and Reuven would say was, "You'll see. You'll see," as they went on dreaming of the day their fortunes were to change forever.

The month of *Sivan* ended and the month of *Tammuz* arrived, finally *Rosh Chadosh* was at hand, but no one came to rent the moon— no one from Chelm, no one from Kotz in the north or Belz in the south, no one at all. What did come, just as it always has and always will, was the new crescent moon, and the good folk of Chelm went out into the fields, already thick with barley, to give thanks and say the Blessing of the New Moon.

"Something's gone wrong," Avrom suggested, trying to keep out of his voice the panic that was swiftly settling in his mind.

"What could go wrong?" asked Reuven, still convinced their plan would work. "There's only one true moon, and we have it locked up. That one in the sky must be an imposter."

"You're probably right," Avrom agreed, "but we'd better check just to be sure."

The brothers gathered up their hammers and crowbar and went out to the shed where they'd hidden the barrel.

"Be careful when you open the lid," Avrom cautioned. "We don't want to let it get away."

They pried the lid off slowly and with great

care, ready to grab the moon if it should try to flee, but when they looked, there was nothing to be seen, only the water that filled the barrel.

"Maybe it sank to the bottom," Reuven offered, with only the slightest glimmer of hope in his voice.

"Let's hope so," Avrom said with a sigh, hoping but not really believing.

They tilted the barrel and poured out the water bit by bit, but there was no sign of the moon—not in the water, not in the barrel, not on the ground.

"It's been stolen!" screamed Avrom.

"It's been stolen!" Reuven joined in.

"Someone stole our moon! Someone stole our moon!" they shouted and cried together.

All this flurry and fuss brought people running. The brothers were hysterical, but eventually they calmed down enough to explain what had happened. They revealed their plan to steal the moon, but instead some scoundrel had stolen it from them.

Now the people of Chelm understood what

the brothers had been babbling about when they said they'd be willing to rent the moon. It wasn't a joke or a riddle at all. It was just one more of Avrom and Reuven's never-ending schemes to get rich.

And from that night on, their inn became known as The Inn of the Stolen Moon, and it will continue to be called that as long as angels have wings.

Reuven's wife, Raisela, was not a dreamer like her husband or her brother-in-law, Avrom. She was practical and orderly, so it was she who took care of most of the business of running the inn.

Raisela was also responsible for the kitchen. She was known far and wide for her culinary skills. In other words, she was a marvelous cook. Her brisket and roast chicken were beyond compare, and her *kugel* and *kreplach* and *tsimmes* were, some said, a taste of Paradise.

Once a lumber merchant traveling to the fir forests of the north stopped at the inn to partake of one of Raisela's meals, and a grand feast it was. When he had finished, he called for the bill so he might be on his way.

"Let's see," said Raisela, "the matzah ball soup, the chopped liver, and the bread come to seven *zlotys*. The roast chicken, the *tsimmes*, and the *helzel*, oh, and let's not forget the honey cakes and tea, come to another seven *zlotys*, which altogether totals eleven *zlotys*."

"I beg your pardon," the lumber merchant said politely, "but seven and seven are fourteen."

"No," insisted Raisela, "seven and seven are eleven."

"Madam, that was such a magnificent meal, one that I'll not soon forget, I wouldn't want to cheat you out of what's rightfully yours. I'll pay you whatever you ask, but where I come from, two times seven are fourteen, not eleven."

"Maybe where you come from it's fourteen," Raisela said, "but here seven and seven are eleven, and I'll prove it to you. My first husband, may he rest in peace, died five years ago, leaving me a widow with four children.

Reuven's wife, may she also rest in peace, also died around that time, leaving him a widower with four children. Sheyne-Lieba, the *shadchen*, the matchmaker, introduced us and we married. Then we were blessed with three children of our own. Now each of us has seven children, and together we have eleven children. So you see, seven and seven are eleven, and that's what you owe me for your meal."

The lumber merchant said nothing further (what could he say?), paid his bill, and continued on his journey to the north. Once again Chelmic logic had triumphed over that of the rest of the world.

Elders and Riddlers

Faivel and Fishel were two of the most respected elders of Chelm. Experienced both in the ways of the world and the ways of wisdom, they each had lived many years and done many things.

Faivel had been a baker and Fishel a tailor, but now that they each had grandchildren and great-grandchildren, their days of labor were behind them.

Much of their time was spent in the Tea House. There they would sit for hours on end, sipping tall glasses of blackberry tea, philosophizing and discussing the state of the world.

"I don't understand," Faivel wondered aloud one day, "why the government makes life so difficult for the poor by taking their last coins for taxes."

"The government needs taxes. Every government collects taxes—always has, always will," Fishel explained.

"But," continued Faivel, "why must the government collect from us? It has a mint of its own. Why can't it simply make as many *zlotys* as it needs?"

"Oh, it could, it could," said Fishel, "but it's just like God and the angels."

"God and the angels? What are you talking about, Reb Fishel?"

"You know, Reb Faivel, that every time a human being does a good deed he creates an angel. Now, God could create all the angels he wants, but he doesn't do so. Why doesn't he? I'll tell you why. He would rather have your angel than his own. It's the same with taxes. Of course the government could produce as many *zlotys* as it likes, but it would much rather have yours."

On another occasion it was Fishel who came up with the question of the day. "Why is it,"

he asked, "that every time you clean something, something else gets dirty? Whereas
whenever you make something dirty, nothing
ever gets clean?"

Since neither he nor his fellow philosopher
were able to unravel the mystery—not even
after three glasses of tea—they decided to set
out on their daily stroll.

It was a bright afternoon in the middle of
summer, but Faivel was carrying an umbrella.
Since the sky was as blue as a thousand robins'
eggs, Fishel thought the umbrella a little odd.
However, Faivel was an eminent Sage like
himself, so surely he must have a good reason.

Suddenly, as if out of nowhere, dark clouds
filled the sky and it began to rain.

"Quick," said Fishel, "put up your umbrella."

"It wouldn't do any good," answered
Faivel.

"What do you mean, it wouldn't do any
good? It's raining cats and dogs."

"It could rain whales and elephants. It still
wouldn't do any good. My umbrella's full of
holes."

"It's full of holes? Then why did you bring it?"

"I didn't think it would rain," Faivel said.

The downpour went as quickly as it came, and Faivel and Fishel continued their stroll through the countryside. They had paused to rest beside a green field where a milk cow was tethered when Faivel slapped his forehead and exclaimed, "Oy! I think I've found a flaw in creation."

"A flaw in creation?" asked his friend incredulously. "What could possibly be wrong with creation?"

"Well," explained Faivel, "take that cow and the birds. Just have a look. The birds are so tiny and their needs are so small—yet God has given them wings so they are able to partake of the bounties of the sky as well as the earth. But the cow, the cow is immense and her needs are great—yet she is bound to the earth. Why didn't God give the cow wings?"

Just then a flock of birds flew directly overhead. One of them responded to the call of nature—*splat!*—right on Faivel's head. He looked up and said, "Aha, I think I know why."

As you might expect, Faivel and Fishel were, like most philosophers, expert riddlers. One of Faivel's favorites was *What do you have that other people use more than you do?*

And a favorite of Fishel's was *What do you have that goes all over the room and never touches anything?*

Actually, these riddles and others like them were favorites among both children and adults because, no matter how difficult they seem at first, it was always possible, with enough thought, to figure out the answer.

Oyzar the Scholar was also a riddler of some note, but his riddles usually made sense *only* after they were explained. Although everyone respected Oyzar for his unique scholarship, there were a few who suggested he spent too much of his time dreaming and that this may have had something to do with the peculiarity of his riddles.

An example: *Why does the dog wag its tail?*

Oyzar's answer: *Because the dog is stronger than the tail. Otherwise, the tail would wag the dog.*

Or: *Why does the hair on a man's head turn gray before the hair in his beard?*

The answer: *Because the hair on his head is at least twenty years older than the hair in his beard.*

Oyzar's own favorite was more complicated.

"What," he would ask, "is green and whistles and hangs on the wall?"

No one was ever able to figure out the answer.

Oyzar, chuckling into his beard—by that time grown long and white—would proclaim, "Why, a herring!"

"A herring?" people would ask in astonishment. "A herring isn't green."

"You could paint it green."

"But a herring doesn't hang on the wall," they argued.

"If you wanted to, you could hang it," explained Oyzar.

"But, but," they would stutter in protest, "there's never been a herring that whistled and there never will be."

"Oh"—Oyzar would laugh triumphantly—"I just threw that in to make it hard."

Oyzar used to ask one even *he* had no answer for: *Why is it that if there's a hole in your shoe, water runs in, but if there's a hole in your pot, the water runs out?*

Oh, you've probably figured out the answers to Faivel's and Fishel's favorite riddles, but just in case . . .

What you have that others use more than you do is your name, and what you have that goes all over the room without touching anything is your voice.

The Feather Merchants

Chelm woke one winter morning to find itself covered in white. It had snowed all through the night and was snowing still. Everything was buried, and no one was going anywhere. Heaven and earth seemed joined together.

Avrom and Reuven sat alone in the main room of the empty inn gazing at the fire, dreaming about the old, waiting for the new. Their most recent venture into the world of commerce had been a true disaster, although neither would admit it.

Months before, at the beginning of autumn, Raisela gave her husband Reuven a large (large for her, at least) sum of money that she had painstakingly saved. She sent him off to the weekly market in Lublin to buy some new pots and pans, some utensils she needed for the kitchen.

It was only natural that Avrom should accompany his brother to the big city, and, as they traveled, it was also only natural that they began to discuss ways they might take that money and turn it into even more.

"What does Raisela need new pots and pans for?" Avrom asked. "She's already the finest cook in all of Chelm. Will new pans make her a better cook?"

"I suppose not," said Reuven, "but she did ask for them, so she must have a good reason."

"I'm sure she does. I'm sure she does," Avrom agreed, "but she doesn't need them today or even tomorrow, does she? Her food will taste just as sweet if she cooks a few more meals in the old pots. If we can invest this money in something and then sell that something for more than we paid for it, we'll have plenty for Raisela's pots and pans and more besides, and with that more we'll be on our way to becoming the rich men we were born to be."

It sounded like a fine idea to Reuven, so when the brothers arrived in Lublin they immediately went to the marketplace, seeking something they could buy low and sell high. They considered stoves. Winter would soon be here, and everyone needed a stove, but on second thought stoves would be far too heavy to carry back to Chelm.

Anvils? Anvils were heavy but much, much lighter than stoves. On third thought, however, no one but blacksmiths used anvils, and Chelm's only blacksmith, Zabalye, already owned three. No, anvils were also out.

The brothers went from stall to stall, shop to shop, store to store. They looked at what the peasants had brought to market in their carts and wagons, all with little success until Reuven called out, "I have it. I have it. We'll buy pillows."

"Pillows? Why pillows?" asked Avrom.

"Well, first of all, pillows are light, certainly lighter than anvils or stoves," Reuven explained. "And besides, who has not heard the saying 'Sleep faster; we need the pillows.' "

"Which must mean," Avrom said excitedly, "that there are simply not enough pillows to go around."

"Exactly the point."

And so the brothers took all of Raisela's pots-and-pans money and invested it in pillows, dozens and dozens and dozens of pillows. Reuven was right about pillows being light, but they are also fluffy, bulky, and unwieldy, particularly if they have to be carried any distance. A man might be able to carry four or five himself or, if he planned meticulously, ten or so strapped to his back, but dozens upon dozens were out of the realm of possibility, as was hiring a wagon to carry them back to Chelm, since they'd spent their very last *zloty* filling out their collection with a tiny pillow for a baby.

There they sat on the edge of the Lublin market with their towering pile of pillows.

The sun was going down in the west. The color of the sky changed from robins' eggs to roses to ashes; a breeze began to blow. Soon it would be dark, and it seemed another of the brothers' schemes was destined for failure. But then the breeze billowed into a wind which blew, of all places, in the direction of Chelm.

At that moment Reuven had another brilliant idea. "There's really no need for *us* to carry these pillows. All we have to do is cut them open and let the wind carry the feathers back to Chelm. Then we gather them up, make them into pillows again, and we'll be rich."

Avrom marveled at his brother's wisdom. Two radiantly remarkable ideas in a single day. This would indeed be a day long remembered in their family history.

They did not hesitate. They slit open the pillows, even the tiny baby one, and cast every last feather into the air, absolutely sure that they'd be borne back to Chelm by the wind.

When the brothers arrived home two days later, the first thing they did was to ask Raisela, "Where did you put all our feathers?"

"Feathers? What feathers?" she asked in

return. "What are you babbling about now? And where are my pots and pans?"

Reuven explained their pillow plan as best he could and tried to calm her with promises of untold riches and more pots and pans than she could use in a lifetime, but Raisela was far too wise and far too experienced to pin her hopes on a whirlwind of feathers flying around God knows where. They could be halfway to America or all the way across Russia for all anyone knew. Pillows indeed!

But Avron and Reuven were certain the feathers would appear.

"Look," Avrom said, "it took us two days to walk from Lublin. It probably takes a feather even longer, especially one that's never been here before."

"If a man can get lost, then surely a feather can lose its way," Reuven added.

Day after day they waited. There was no sign of their feathers, not even a speck of down.

"Could they have been stolen? No. A moon can be stolen. A pillow can be stolen. But zillions and zillions of feathers? Never."

"Perhaps the wind stopped to rest. Perhaps it grew tired carrying all those feathers."

Perhaps, but when the Sabbath came and went, the brothers felt they had to do something. Each day they walked to the outskirts of Chelm to await their feathers and their fortune. They even put signs up along the road:

FEATHERS! →THIS WAY TO
AVROM AND REUVEN

Weeks passed. Months. *Rosh Hashanah, Yom Kippur, Succoth.* The leaves of the oak turned from green to gold and began to fall to the ground. The apples were picked and packed away in straw-filled barrels. Only a few still hung on the trees along the orchards' edges, left there for any beggars or wanderers who might pass by. The grain and potatoes, the beets and cabbages had been harvested and stored in root cellars.

And still not a single hint of a single feather.

Now winter was upon them, and as the

snow continued to fall, Avrom and Reuven sat side by side, silently staring into the fire, each thinking his own thoughts, which, not surprisingly, were the same thoughts: *Maybe the feathers are buried under the snow. Maybe they're hibernating like the bears. Maybe they'll come in the spring.*

Maybe. Maybe not. The last I heard, Avrom and Reuven were still waiting with perfect faith and hope for their feathers to arrive and make them rich.

And who knows? Perhaps someday they will.

The Council of
Seven Sages

By now it should be clear that everyone in Chelm was steeped in the ways of wisdom.

Yet wise as Chelmites were, a special group of Sages was needed to guide the community through the *most* perplexing problems and quandaries. When the rabbi had no answer, when Oyzar the Scholar could not come up with a solution, when those most respected elders, Faivel and Fishel, were unable to unravel the complexities of the situation, the people always turned to the Council of Seven Sages—the wisest of the wise, one for each day of the week.

For example, when the question was

raised, which is more important, the sun or the moon, all of Chelm divided into two camps. Those who felt the sun was more important were just as passionate as those who felt the moon was more important. Households opposed households, husbands argued with wives, children disagreed with their parents. Just as the entire community was about to come to blows, the Council of Seven Sages took the question under consideration. That was, after all, what they were there for.

For seven days and seven nights the Council met and pondered. They discussed, deliberated, and dissected the question and finally announced their decision: clearly it was the moon, because the moon shines at night when we need the light the most, whereas the sun shines during the day when we already have plenty of light.

The Council was also able, after much musing, to clear up a mystery that has baffled great minds for centuries—that is, why is it cold in the winter and hot in the summer?

Once again, the problem was so complex

the Council needed seven days and seven nights before they could present their answer to the rest of the community with absolute confidence.

Using their brilliant collective knowledge, they explained that during the winter we light our stoves, which, in turn, heat the air around us. Gradually, all the air gets warmer and warmer until, by the time summer arrives, the air has become very hot.

Naturally, we don't want the air to get any hotter, God forbid, so we stop lighting our stoves. Gradually the air cools down until, by the time winter arrives, the air is freezing. That's when we begin to light our stoves, and the process starts all over again.

Once there was a murder in Chelm. Yes, a murder, just as they have in Warsaw or Moscow or New York.

It happened like this. Selig the Winemaker drank too much of his own wine and, in a fit of drunken passion, killed a fellow Chelmite.

He was brought before the Council of Seven Sages. There had been many witnesses, and Selig did not deny what he had done, nor did he say anything in his own defense. The Council had no choice but to declare him guilty and sentence him to be hanged.

That seemed to settle the matter until Avrom rose in the courtroom and addressed the Council. "Honorable Sages," he said. "It is true that Selig has committed a terrible crime and his sentence is a proper one. However, the Council has failed to take into account an important practical consideration. Selig is our only winemaker. There is not another one within a hundred miles. If we hang him, where will we get our wine?"

For a moment there was a heavy silence as everyone considered the question. Then, almost in unison, a dozen voices cried, "Indeed, indeed, where will we get our wine?"

Some of the Seven Sages were among those asking the question, so they continued their deliberations until they ultimately came up with a revised verdict.

"Since we have only one winemaker, it would be a great wrong against the community to deprive everyone of his skills. Still, justice must be done, and since we have more than enough cobblers, it is decreed that one of them shall be hanged instead."

As wise as the Council of Seven Sages was, there are two questions about which they were never able to come to a consensus, and that remain unsettled to this day.

The first concerns how human beings grow. Do they grow from the head up, or do they grow from the feet down?

Those who favored the feet-down theory presented their own experience of growth as proof. When they were young, they said, the day came when they were given their first pair of long pants. Inevitably the pants were so long they dragged on the ground; but as they grew, some faster than others, the pants kept rising until the bottoms were well above their ankles—which proves conclusively that a human being grows from the feet down.

There were, however, other members of the Council who, with just as much conviction, insisted it's the other way around. They steadfastly maintained that we grow from our heads up and offered equally convincing proof on their behalf.

All you need do, they said, is look carefully at a group of marching soldiers. At the bottom their feet are all the same, on the same level. But when you look at their heads, you'll see that some are higher than others, some lower—which demonstrates that we grow from the head up.

The other question that even the deepest thinkers of Chelm were never able to agree on has to do with a simple piece of bread and butter. Butter was considered a special treat, so the children were cautioned to be extra careful whenever they were fortunate enough to receive any. If they dropped a slice of buttered bread, they were warned, it would always fall buttered side down.

This had been an accepted truth in Chelm for as long as anyone could remember, until the youngest three of the Seven Sages decided to look into the matter. They discussed, deliberated, and dissected, not for seven days and seven nights or even seven weeks but for seven months. When they announced their conclusion, it created an uproar.

It was not true, they claimed, that a piece of buttered bread always falls buttered side down. To prove it, they would conduct a public scientific experiment.

The town square was filled with seekers of truth that day. They came from miles around.

The three young Sages mounted a platform especially built for the experiment. It stood above the crowd so everyone would be able to see the demonstration with their own eyes. One of the Sages held the bread and one held the butter while the third held a knife, with which he slowly and deliberately buttered the bread.

Next, Kopel the Candlemaker, an ordinary citizen, was called forward. He was asked to hold the bread with the buttered side facing the blue sky and then to drop it. The crowd was hushed as Kopel took the bread. He held it for a moment. The butter began to melt. He dropped it.

The bread fell buttered side down.

"Aha," shouted the four oldest Sages, who had been standing to the side of the platform. "It fell buttered side down. That proves we were right all along."

"All it proves," responded the would-be scientists, "is that we buttered the wrong side."

Every once in a while the Council of Seven Sages would repeat the experiment, but no matter which side the bread fell on some of them would insist that the wrong side had been buttered.

Now that you know how the people of Chelm thought and what makes them so wise, I leave you to answer these two vital questions—about how people grow and about how buttered bread falls—for yourself.

Before you're tempted to say, "But I'm no fool," I would urge you to remember what the good folk of Chelm always said: *If you claim you are not a fool, you only show your ignorance, for is it not written that "the world was delivered into the hands of fools"?*

And *I* ask you, is this not the world?

AFTERWORD

I

For as long as I can remember knowing anything, I remember knowing about Chelm and its silly citizens.

I was a very young boy when I heard my first Chelm stories from my grandfather—may his memory be a blessing. He had come to this country from Lithuania near the end of the last century seeking a better life, a life free from *pogroms*, persecution, and poverty.

He had been a baker's apprentice in Vilna, and he continued to follow the baker's trade here in the United States. He was a fine, fine baker, but what he loved to do most of all was tell stories—all kinds of stories. There were stories about great leaders like Abraham and Moses and stories about courageous heroes and heroines like Judah Maccabee and Queen Esther. He told stories of demons and imps, rabbis and holy men, czars and empresses of the distant and not-so-distant past.

Among his favorites were those about the good and decent folk of Chelm. They soon became favorites of mine also, because not only did I hear them from him but from my mother and father, aunts, uncles, cousins, and teachers as well. Often when I said or did something foolish, at least in the eyes of a grown-up, I was told, "Don't be a *Chelmer chochem*. Don't act like a fool from Chelm."

For me Chelm was as real as Hollywood or Antarctica, Krypton or Metropolis, New Orleans or Oz. Faivel and Fishel were no less a part of my life than the Lone Ranger and Tonto.

As a storyteller I've been telling these tales for decades. Listeners frequently ask where they can find them in print. When I realized there was no single source currently available that captured the delightfully unique character of the Chelmites, I decided it was time to commit these stories to paper.

It would be a simple task, I thought. After all, I knew them well. They've been a part of my life for almost half a century. However, once I began to record them, I discovered that, although I knew the Chelmites and their ways intimately, I really didn't know much about *where* they lived.

Were the mountains around Chelm the same as the mountains I now live in? Were they rough and jagged or had they been worn smooth by thousands of years of snow and rain? What kinds of mushrooms grow in the forests? What birds sing at twilight? There were many questions that could be answered only by going to the places where these stories were born.

It became clear that a journey to Eastern Europe would be necessary to learn about the trees and flowers, to experience sunrises and sunsets, to feel the rain, to walk in the mud.

II

Almost every culture has its fools or group of fools who are there to help us laugh when we need to the most. Sometimes it's an individual like Jean Sot in France or Silly Jack in England. Sometimes it's an entire town of fools like Schildburg in Germany or Montieri in Italy. For the Greeks it's Abdera; for the English, Gotham; and for the Jews it's Chelm.

No one knows how long people have been telling stories about the Sages (or Fools) of Chelm. Some folklore scholars say five hundred years, others say longer, but just about everyone agrees that the stories originated and developed in the Yiddish-speaking world of Eastern Europe.

Through the years the borders have changed continually. What was once Poland is now part of Russia. What was once Galicia is now part of Poland. But at one time more than seven million Jews lived in a territory that stretched from the Black Sea in the south to the Baltic Sea in the north, from the plains of Germany in the west to the Caucasus Mountains of Russia in the east.

Eastern Europe was once the inspired, vital center of Jewish life and thought, faith, religion, and culture, flourishing from as early as the tenth century until the Nazis appeared in our own century and tried to destroy it forever.

I went there, I think, without illusions. I was well aware of my people's history. I knew that six million of them, along with millions of others, had been murdered during those brutal years some call World War II and others call the Holocaust. I certainly didn't go expecting to find the living, vibrant world of my grandfathers, but I was not prepared for the total absence and denial of the life that had once been there.

I spent most of my time traveling in Poland, from East Germany to the Ukraine and back again. One branch of my family had lived and worked in and around Warsaw for three generations, and there were once, in my own lifetime, three and a half million Jews living in Poland.

Now there are less than three thousand, and they are mostly old and isolated. Signs of Jewish life are almost nonexistent. Only a few synagogues still stand. The Jewish cemeteries are difficult, if not impossible, to find; they are generally in the final stages of vanishing, either because of neglect (there's simply no one left to care for them) or, worse, because of anti-Semitic desecrations. The monuments and museums at concentration camps like Majdanek and Treblinka barely mention the fact that so many Jews died there. And in the woods, at places like Belzec and Sobibor, where almost no one ever goes, are mounds of the bones and ashes of the victims, bearing silent witness to the monstrous crimes committed there.

III

The broken leg I received at the hands of two thugs along the banks of the romantic and heavily polluted Vistula River in the center of ancient Cracow was not the most important part of my trip, only the most dramatic. Those young hoodlums were, after all, only seeking my money, but the incident and the six painful days it took me to return home and get proper medical attention have come to symbolize for me the difficulties of the journey *and* of keeping these stories alive.

What began as a simple research trip became a journey of the soul, a return to the self, if you will. It became a deeply moving voyage of discovery, one that, among other things, showed me again how necessary a sense of humor is if we are to do more than survive in this world.

These stories about Chelm have been told by the Jewish people during both good times and terrible times. In the best of times, we're able to laugh together. In the worst of times, the innocent stupidity and sweetness of the Chelmites speaks of a universal quality we all recognize and are able to smile at—if only inwardly, if only for a fleeting second.

And it is this smile that connects us to the past and to the future. It is this smile that keeps us human.

IV

Along the way I actually did visit a town called Chelm. It is a lovely place situated, not deep in a valley as is the Chelm of legend, but high in the Lublin Uplands with a sweeping view of the surrounding countryside.

It was late autumn. The maples and oaks were ablaze with their new coats of red and yellow leaves. Each evening at sunset it seemed as if entire hillsides were on fire. Except for the last turnips, most of the crops were safely stored away, while the freshly turned fields waited patiently for the nourishment of the first snows.

Red geraniums, white chrysanthemums, pink hollyhocks, and purple asters filled window boxes and gardens. The woods were alive with mushrooms of every shape, every size, every color. Each morning, mist rose from the forest floor but was gone by the time people left their homes on their way to work or to market.

The first Jewish settlers had arrived there almost a thousand years ago. They came to work in the logging and lumber business made possible by the huge forests to the north and east. Less than fifty years ago there were fifteen thousand Jews living in Chelm, almost half the population, but today, among its seventy thousand inhabitants, there are none, absolutely none. They have all disappeared. Most were brutally murdered at the killing camp called Sobibor, located only thirty miles to the northeast. The few that did survive have long ago moved on to new lives elsewhere.

Only a handful of the old people in Chelm remember, or admit to remembering, their onetime neighbors, and none of them know these stories.

Of course, the Chelm of our stories is not the Chelm that today is known in Poland for its shoes and its cement. It never was, even when it sparkled and teemed with Jewish life. Just as nobody knows when these stories began, no one knows how Chelm came to be known as the town of fools.

Our Chelm is the Chelm of the spirit and imagination that has existed, generation after generation, in the minds and hearts of those who've told and listened to these tales.

Our Chelm is a magical place filled with honest and righteous men and women for whom the idea of defeat passes as quickly as a gaggle of geese flying south.

Our Chelm has "a soul which yearns for beauty, which is full of mercy, which possesses faith, which seeks justice."*

Chelm is where hopes and dreams and laughter go on living—and will go on living as long as you and I go on telling these stories.

STEVE SANFIELD
Montezuma Hill, California
Rosh Hashanah 5751 / Autumn 1990

*Yisroel Aschendorf in *The Commemoration Book of Chelm*. M. Bakal-czuk-Felin, ed. Johannesburg: Former Residents of Chelm, 1954.

GLOSSARY

aleph-beys First two letters of the Hebrew/
Yiddish alphabet. Same as ABC's.

Bar Mitzvah The ceremony, held in a synagogue, in which a thirteen-year-old boy
reaches the status of manhood and as-
sumes the rights and obligations of an
adult.

Chanukah The Festival of Lights. An eight-
day winter celebration commemorating
the rededication of the Temple in Jerusa-
lem by the Maccabees after their victory
over Syrian despots in 167 B.C.E.

Chelmer chochem Literally "a Sage, or wise
man, of Chelm," but when used sarcasti-
cally, it means a fool.

Days of Awe The ten-day period of soul-searching and reflection that begins on *Rosh Hashanah* and culminates in *Yom Kippur*.

helzel A delicacy made by stuffing the neck of a goose, chicken, or duck with meal, egg, and spices.

kreplach A dumpling of chopped meat or cheese usually served in soup. Called *wonton* in China.

kugel Noodle or bread pudding generally cooked with raisins.

L'chayim "To life." A popular and traditional toast.

Mazel tov "Good luck." Congratulations.

mikva A ritual bathhouse and a necessary part of traditional communities.

Passover An eight-day spring festival commemorating the exodus of the ancient Hebrew people from their slavery in Egypt.

Pesach "Passover."

pogrom An organized attack or persecution, often officially encouraged, particularly against the Jews.

Purim   Festival of Lots marking the triumph over the Persian Haman's plot to exterminate the Jews. Noted for its gaiety, masquerades, and festive meal.

Rosh Chadosh   "Head of the Month." First day of each Jewish month.

Rosh Hashanah   Jewish New Year. Arrives in the fall, usually in September.

schlemiel   A clumsy, inept person. A schlemiel will throw a drowning man a rope—both ends.

Shabbes   The Sabbath, the holiest day of the week, traditionally devoted to rest, study, prayer, and family. An island in time when every man and woman can become a king and queen and every boy and girl a prince and princess. Begins at sunset on Friday and ends at sunset on Saturday.

shadchen   A professional matchmaker.

shammes   The sexton, caretaker of a synagogue; the rabbi's personal attendant.

shul   Synagogue. The center of Jewish communal life, where people meet, pray, study, debate, and argue.

Sivan and **Tammuz**   The ninth and tenth months, respectively, of the Jewish year. Midsummer.

Succoth   An autumn harvest festival.

Talmud   "Teaching." A vast record of discussions and commentaries, recorded over many centuries, dealing with law, ethics, traditions, and ceremony.

Torah   "The Law." The Pentateuch, or Five Books of Moses, but also refers to the practice and teachings of Judaic law in general.

tsimmes   A sweet dish in which carrots, prunes, and/or sweet potatoes are mixed with honey and spices and left to cook slowly for many hours.

Yom Kippur   Day of Atonement. The most solemn and sacred day of the year, spent in fasting and prayer.

zloty   A large, silver coin, generally worth as little as a penny and as much as a quarter, depending on the time and place of its use.

BIBLIOGRAPHY

Should you be interested in seeing how other writers and storytellers have chosen to tell some of these and other stories of Chelm, the following books in English are recommended.

Ausubel, Nathan, ed. *A Treasury of Jewish Folklore*. New York: Crown Publishers, 1948.

Browne, Lewis. *The Wisdom of Israel*. New York: Random House, 1945. Reprinted as *Wisdom of the Jewish People*. Northvale, N.J.: Jason Aronson, Inc., 1988.

Freedman, Florence B. *It Happened in Chelm: A Story of the Legendary Town of*

Fools. New York: Shampolsky Publishers, 1990.

Howe, Irving, and Eliezer Greenberg, eds. *A Treasury of Yiddish Stories*. New York: Viking Press, 1953. Revised and updated edition. New York: Viking Penguin, 1990.

Jagendorf, M. A. *Noodlehead Stories from Around the World*. New York: The Vanguard Press, 1957.

Leach, Maria. *Noodles, Nitwits, and Numskulls*. Cleveland: World Publishing, 1961. Paperback reprint. New York: Dell Yearling, 1979.

Novak, William, and Moshe Waldoks, eds. *The Big Book of Jewish Humor*. New York: Harper & Row, 1981.

Pavlàt, Leo. *Jewish Folktales*. London: Beehive Books, 1986.

Richman, Jacob. *Jewish Wit and Wisdom*. New York: Padres Publishing House, 1952.

————. *Laughs from Jewish Lore*. New York: Hebrew Publishing Company, 1954.

Roskies, Diane K., and David G. Roskies. *The Shtetl Book*. Hoboken, N.J.: KTAV Publishing House, Inc., 1975.

Schwartz, Amy. *Yossel Zissel and the Wisdom of Chelm.* Philadelphia: The Jewish Publication Society, 1986.

Serwer, Blanche Luria. *Let's Steal the Moon: Jewish Tales Ancient and Recent.* Boston: Little, Brown and Company, 1970. Paperback reprint. New York: Shampolsky Publishers, 1987.

Simon, Solomon. *The Wise Men of Chelm and Their Merry Tales.* New York: Behrman House, 1945.

———. *More Wise Men of Chelm and Their Merry Tales.* New York: Behrman House, 1965.

Singer, Isaac Bashevis. *The Fools of Chelm and Their History.* New York: Farrar, Straus & Giroux, 1968.

———. *Stories for Children.* New York: Farrar, Straus & Giroux, 1984.

———. *Zlateh the Goat and Other Stories.* New York: Harper & Row, 1966.

Spaulding, Henry D. *Encyclopedia of Jewish Humor.* New York: Johnathan David Publishers, 1969.

Tenenbaum, Samuel. *The Wise Men of*

Chelm. New York: Thomas Yoseloff, Publisher, 1965. Paperback reprint. New York: Collier Books, 1969.

Weinreich, Beatrice Silverman, ed. *Yiddish Folktales*. New York: Pantheon Books/Yivo Institute for Jewish Research, 1988.